They Call Me

AFRICA

BY NADINE A. LUKE
ILLUSTRATED BY SAMEER KASSAR

Library of Congress Control Number:
2020918857

Hardcover ISBN: 978-1-7350635-4-6
Paperback ISBN: 978-1-7350635-5-3

Dedication

This book is dedicated to every child that has ever experienced the ugly faces of racism and bullying. Remember, you know who you are and the greatness that is within you. Always let your light shine above their hatred and ignorance.

My name is Amiri. I have dark brown skin and brown eyes. My hair is styled in locs. Though I am very smart, at times I have to think longer than others to decide the correct words I want to say. When my words come out, they are sometimes muffled because of a slight speech impediment.

Looking and speaking this way had never been a problem for me until the day I entered third grade. I was excited to go to school. My locs had just been retwisted the night before, I had on my brand new school clothes, and I was feeling great! I walked into the classroom with a big smile, ready to start my day.

As I passed a few of the desks to find the one with my name on it, some of the students pointed at me and whispered. I looked around me and behind me, but I was the only one standing there. That's when someone yelled out, "Hey, look at Africa!" Everyone started laughing. Another boy yelled, "Look at his hair. It looks like he has a head full of worms!" My heart sank! I didn't understand why they were saying these things.

People I thought were my friends from last year laughed along with the two new boys who were leading the crowd. As I took my seat, I heard one of the girls say, "Wow, he does look like Africa. Look how black he is. Why is he even here?"

Finally, the teacher told everyone to settle down and stop. Though the voices stopped, the whispers and hidden pointing did not. I didn't understand why they pointed and laughed at me. I liked my hair and my skin.

All of a sudden my heart started hurting and I felt a drop of water come from my eyes. I thought, "Oh no! I can't let anyone see me cry or they will really come after me." I bent down like I was tying my shoe and quickly wiped my eyes before anyone could see the tears.

Though my teacher was talking about my favorite subject, science, I really couldn't concentrate because I could not stop thinking about my classmates calling me Africa and saying I was too black and that my hair looked like worms.

When it was time to go home, one of the students dropped a picture on my desk of a boy colored in with a black crayon with what looked like brown worms on his head. The writing said, "Hey Africa! LOL."

When my parents picked my sisters and me up from school, they asked each of us how our day went. I just said, "Okay," and was silent all the way home. When we got there, I told them I was tired and wanted to go to bed.

They asked me if everything was okay. I said, "Yes," and then asked, "Do we have any books on Africa?" They told me that there were plenty on the bookshelf in the family room.

So, that's when I started my quest to find out just what Africa was about since so many kids at school thought my name was Africa.

When I went back to school the next day, it was the same thing, only now more people joined in with teasing me about my skin, hair, and calling me Africa.

I told the teacher and she tried to help. They just stopped saying it where the teacher could hear, but they continued to torment me in class, on the yard during recess, and in the cafeteria during lunch.

I felt miserable.

Some of my friends from last year tried to help too by telling these bullies to leave me alone. That just made the bullies start bullying them as well, calling them "Losers with Africa!"

Each day I went home, I read more and more about Africa. I found out that Africa is one of the riches continents in the world.

The first multi-genius who looked just like me was from Africa.

I finally decided to tell my parents about everything that was happening at school and how I decided I would stand up to the bullies. They were surprised that I hadn't told them about it sooner, but they were proud because I was able to come up with a solution.

I decided to wear one of my traditional outfits my parents got from Ghana, West Africa to school the next day.

When I walked into the classroom someone yelled, "Hey, look! Africa is here!" I looked around the room and said, "Yes, I am! Thank you for recognizing my greatness!"

Someone else yelled, "Did you feed your worms today?" I replied, "Thank you for noticing my locs, which is the preferred hair style of ancient African Royalty, including the Pharaohs!"

They looked at each other and tried to figure out what was going on.

Another student yelled out, "Your skin is so dark, if we turned off the lights we couldn't see you."

My response was, "Did you know the melanin in my skin protects me from the dangerous effects of the sun? and that I am the same color as Imhotep, one of the smartest men to ever walk the planet?

When you call me Africa and talk about my skin and hair you are affirming that you see greatness in me because Africa is one of the greatest continents in the world. It is the cradle of civilization, science, math, language and engineering.

It is home to some of the most precious jewels, metals, and natural medicines.

So, when you call me Africa, understand that I know who I am and I will not allow anyone to use racism and bully me to become who I am not! By this time, everyone, including the teacher, was listening--even though I said it in my special muffled way.

The room went completely silent and then my teacher started applauding. "Amiri, I am so proud of you," she said. Many of the students clapped too.

When I got home, I couldn't wait to tell my parents what happened and how everything was different in class, at recess, and at lunch. The bullies were silent and I was loving school again. My parents and sisters gave me big hugs.

My dad said, "We have always known that greatness lies in you. That is why we named you Amiri. It means *African Prince and Ruler*. We are so happy you have embraced it as well. Yes, you are Africa!"

Made in the USA
Monee, IL
18 October 2021